Owyn

hidden journals volume 4

Owyn hidden journals volume 4

Author's Disclaimer

This book is entirely fictional. Any characters or events are purely figments of the author's imagination. The city of St. Augustine isn't fictional and is in northern Florida. Many of the businesses and locations mentioned in the book can be found there. No part of this publication may be reproduced, transmitted or redistributed either in its entirety or in part without the author's express written consent.

Other books by Elle

The Bloodseekers: St. Augustine Novellas
The Vampires Next Door Book 1
The Monster Upstairs Book 2
The Ghost Within Book 3

hidden journals
Isandro
Alarico
Cayto
Owyn

Zombie Girl
Premonition Book 1
Infection Book 2
Retribution Book 3

Baby Girl
In the Beginning Volume 1
Moonlighting in Paris Volume 2
City by the Bay Volume 3
Bite the Big Apple Volume 4
Caribbean Heat Volume 5
Return to the Bay Volume 6
Prison of the Past Volume 7
Baby Girl Box Set - Volumes 1-4

Owyn hidden journals volume 4

preface

The world peaceful and the magic balanced, the Slayers moved on with their lives. They finished high school, went to college, and started careers. By thirty they realized they weren't aging. People were beginning to notice. It was time to leave their present lives. Mandy and the wolves went to Wolf Manor and she started an ecommerce store selling herbal remedies that she spelled with healing magic. Vicky traveled the world working as a freelance photographer and journalist. Opal and Rylan settled in his home country of Spain, in the mountains, where she took an interest in antiques. Lacey worked her way up in the fashion design world, started her own line, and designed on the move. Adrian wrote code and designed video games from home. Rodham and Alison started an online bookstore. It was her idea. The plan was to have a child when the business got off the ground but that didn't happen; maybe fertility was impossible with their immortal bodies. They stayed hidden and kept themselves out of the public eye, but that grew old.

After Opal's parents' deaths they settled into her home in St. Augustine. With Opal's interest in antiques, Alison's in literature they opened an antique store -- Relics in historical St. Augustine -- and they blended into the mystery and paranormal shroud of the city.

St. Augustine had grown, but the historic area was still cryptic and filled with the same legends of the past as if it was molded in time. Alison was never able to remove the spell on Alistair and invited him to live with them. The others were a bit unnerved by someone they couldn't see living with them, and maybe a boggart was a dangerous entity to have around. It turned out his curious nature discovered the secrets of the house. They were hidden in the walls and beneath the floorboards. This is one of the hidden journals he found.

chapter 1

"**I** cannot believe my brother will be a married man tomorrow," Horacio drawled as we staggered home. He wasn't my blood brother but my brother in friendship. We grew up together.

"It'll happen to you one day," I assured him.

He wrapped a thin brown arm around my neck. "I would need a lady to court for that to happen." He spent more time studying than with the ladies, even with his fine good looks. I was the rugged one with uncontrollable hair and had to shave twice a day to keep my face smooth.

A gust of wind from the Bay blew through the alley. The streetlamps stuttered then flickered back. "My friend, any woman would be lucky." He was more a scientist than a family man. One who treated the sick.

He stopped and dropped his arm from my shoulder and faced me. His dark eyes fixed on mine. "I will live through you. Your children will be mine. Yes?" His lips turned up in a smile.

A strong wind rushed through the alley, knocking us nearly to our knees and blowing out the streetlamps. Carried on it, the smell of death. Two figures descended before us. We steadied ourselves and stepped backwards towards the brick wall of a building.

Their forms silhouetted by moonlight. They were tall with stretched faces and pointy ears on the sides of their heads. Their fingers adorned with claw-like projections and the source of a stench. I slid my hand slowly to my waist where I kept a knife my father had given me. It was made of bone. I tapped Horacio with my elbow to get his attention.

He was fixed on the inhuman creatures before us. They were like something out of this world. A combination of human and demon. I tapped him harder, but he was fixated on them. Anxiety wedged itself into my gut, gnawing at the lining. Something inside me was trying to break free.

Horacio stepped forward. In the moment, my thought was saving my brother from the spell the demons cast on him. I gripped the knife and pulled it from my waist. Thrusting an arm in front of Horacio, I pushed him back, forcing him into the wall behind us. "What have you done to him?!"

"That knife will not harm us," one of the demons seethed, coming closer. Its lips an unearthly gray.

I stepped in front of Horacio, the blade shining in the moonlight. "I think it will." My father's words when he gave me the knife were: 'This is made from the bones of demon hunters. One strike and they will wither and die.'

"We do not fear you *lobo*!" Their voices chorused in the night, riding on the wind.

The rising beast inside me challenged them: "Come closer and we will see."

"You cannot take us all," said another voice, a female, from my left. Her lanky, shapeless body and grayish skin made her almost indistinguishable from the male. I turned to see three more demons on us.

They were right, I couldn't take them all, but I would try and die fighting. I waved the knife from side to side. "Stay back!" I warned.

A roar sounded as the earth trembled beneath my feet and, from out of nowhere, another creature appeared with the body of a human but the snout of a wolf. A mixture of fur and hair bulging from beneath its clothes. It jumped on one of the demons, sinking its teeth into its neck. Black webbed from the bite and spread over the demon, smoke pouring from its extremities. It fell to the ground, writhing in pain, its screams piercing my ears as it burst into flames.

The demons surrounded the wolf-like creature as it snapped its jaws at them, standing on all fours. Its arms and legs human, but its feet and hands like paws. It growled as it stepped over the dying demon as if daring them to come closer. *Was this a demon hunter?* Surely it was. To fight something inhuman one would have to be inhuman too.

The demons swarmed the wolf man as he threw them from his back and snapped at them. My head became dizzy and my hands shook, but not in fear. Something inside me was fighting to free itself. I lost my balance and stumbled to the ground. My hand losing its grip on the knife that crashed to the ground with me.

It was in that moment that something grabbed Horacio. I turned my head as two demons sank their jagged, moonlight-bathed into his neck. One on each side. "No!" I hollered in the surrounding air at no one and everyone then grabbed the knife from the ground and plunged it into the demon's leg. Black blood bubbled through its pants and drained down its leg as it crumpled to the ground, writhing in agony as flames consumed him.

I slashed at the other, but it moved quicker than my hand.

Horacio collapsed into a heap, blood coursing from his neck. "Brother, no!" I screamed, ripping my shirt and tying it around the bites on each side of his neck. Holding his head in my lap, tears formed in my eyes as I looked into the golden-brown eyes of the wolf man. Familiarity sparkled, but in my distress and pain I didn't make the connection until it was too late.

They had pinned him to the ground as he continued to snap and fight against them. A sword with an orange stone in the hilt swung across the neck of a demon, lopping it off. It dropped, and so did its body, with a thud. The sword belonged to a young man, his eyes radiating an identical shade of orange. His skin tan like Horacio's.

A tall, dark woman ran into the alley, her sword glowing emerald green, followed by a young man wielding a glowing blue sword. *If the wolf man was a demon hunter, then what were these new fighters? What was I in the middle of?*

Demon heads flew and the wolf man lay on the ground, his back to me. His feet no longer wolf paws but human. The fur/hair replaced with curly human hair. He turned his head and faced me. "Owyn," he said breathlessly.

"Father?" Confused and distraught, I didn't understand. *How could he be something more than human?* Yes, we were hairy folk and bulky, but never did I think… How? I'd ponder that question for years. Laying Horacio's head on the ground I crawled to the man who'd cared for me on his own my entire youth. My mother died in childbirth. My callused hands were proof of the carpentry trade he taught me. *How could he be a wolf man or demon hunter?* It didn't register as I crawled to him. The battle between the demons and colorful sworded slayers raged around us.

"Father." I took his head in my hands and leaned over him, tears falling from my eyes. Human or not, he was my father. I swallowed. "You're going to be OK. I'm taking you home."

"No, son, I am dying. You must kill Horacio or he will become one of them." The words stabbed through my heart as if someone jabbed a sword through it.

There was no way. He was my brother, and innocent. I'd find a way to use his medicine to save him. I had to, or at least try. "No, not him. He is kind, he is gentle. No!" I couldn't wrap my mind around what was happening and lost awareness of the battle. It was only me and my father in that moment.

He choked and swallowed. "Son, take your knife and strike Horacio, then free the beast inside…" He coughed, blood bubbling from his mouth. "You." His body went limp as his dead eyes stared into mine.

"Father!" I screamed in anguish. Rage raced through my extremities. My blood boiled and a ferociousness I'd never known took control. I clutched the knife in my shaking hand as I crawled to Horacio.

Gray fur moved up my arms, then vanished inside my pores. My face tingled as I reached Horacio. He lay peacefully where I left him. Blood soaked the cloth around his neck, poured and puddled around his head. Each of his breaths a struggle. There was no way I could save him; he'd lost far too much blood.

My father's words echoed in my head. He loved Horacio like a son and wouldn't ask me to do this if there was another option. I grabbed the hilt of the bone knife with both hands and sunk it into my friend's chest.

His body convulsed as blackness took over it. Every emotion I'd ever felt brimmed inside me as my nose no longer tingled, fur no longer erupted and receded from my skin. Paws claimed my hands and feet. Clothes ripped from my body. Sound worked its way through my voice box erupting as a woeful howl into the moonlit night.

chapter 2

What should have been a pivotal moment of happiness turned into the moment my life was destroyed and sheer sadness. Through the window I took one last glance at my sleeping bride-to-be — Portencia. Her golden hair splayed on the pillow. I thought of the last time I held her in my arms. Her warm breath against my neck and the baby soft skin of her hand in mine.

I was a hideous monster. There was no way I could possibly live a normal life and I couldn't bring her pain and shame. Into what was left of the night, I ran off in wolf form far away from St. Augustine. My mind a flurry of thoughts and guilt for leaving my father and best friend, but what choice did I have?

I fell asleep and woke as a human again, lying naked amongst the trees of a dense forest. The highest branches reached into the sky and touched the clouds.

It was there I made a clearing and used the wood and the carpentry skills my father taught me and built a home, but it was never finished, always calling to me and after years I had a mansion in the trees. Three stories high with a balcony on each level.

Building kept the beast inside me tame and controlled. It kept me from thinking about that night.

Every time I did, my body tingled and fur erupted and receded. So I built and cut down trees, taking my frustration out on the forest and guiding my love for all those I lost that night into finely crafted beams and frames.

I lived off the land, hunting, and eating the apples provided by the natural grove. They were the most sweet and delicious apples I'd ever tasted. For goods, I traded furs. It was a lonely existence, but I was hidden. My worst fear that I owned after several years was my fear of harming someone. In wolf form, I didn't have full control. I was an animal, hunted like an animal, and ran far, always waking naked outside my home. *What if my wolf self was capable of killing humans?*

At first, I fought the battle to change, unwilling to accept the beast in me, but overtime I gave in and allowed it one night a month — the full moon. On that night each month I allowed my sorrow to consume me as my body transformed into a wild animal. My home had to be the most remote spot on the planet, which made it perfect for the monster I was.

In the evenings when the sun fell, I whittled. Pictures, silverware, plates, bowls from wood and the bones of my prey. Built furniture with my hands. The rooms were empty, and my voice and pain echoed inside the walls. I stopped counting time. It had no meaning. I would live and die alone at the edge of the world.

One fall night, the neighing from a horse woke me from a sound slumber. I jolted from bed and peered out the window. Animals didn't venture close to the house. I figured it was because I marked it during my outings as a wolf. Nothing was there. Falling back into sleep I woke again when light streamed through the window and beckoned my eyes to open.

I scooped a heaping ladle of stew from the pit hanging in the hearth into a large bowl and drank the last of the stream water. Today I would get more. My belly filled, I set out with empty buckets hanging from my shoulder pole and a bowl in my hands for apples.

When I approached the stream, my eyes couldn't believe what they were seeing. The horse from my dreams was there drinking the water. I gently placed the large bowl on the earth and lifted the pole from my shoulder, placing it on the ground next to the bowl. He lifted his head and acknowledged me as I moved closer, taking easy steps. His eyes never left me as I approached him.

His body covered in brown hair, with a black mane and tail. I reached my hand towards him and touched his head. He was tame and his mane and tail tangle-free as if recently brushed. He was cared for. My eyes scanned the area. I listened with my extra-sensory hearing, but there was no sound belonging to a human, no breathing, running, leaves rustling underfoot. I swallowed. The trickle of water through the stream, turning of rocks and dirt, and the rustle of leaves from the breeze filled my ears.

Somehow he'd gotten loose and run far. He would come in handy for my trips to trade. I filled the water buckets and reached for the bowl, carrying it to the apple grove. The horse watched by his spot at the stream as I claimed a bowl full of fresh, sweet apples. I brought one back to him. He ate it from my hand, tickling my palm with the whiskers around his mouth.

Once again, I lifted the pole around my shoulders, careful not to spill, grabbed my bowl and headed back. After several moments, he trotted behind me. A smile crept over my face. Possibly because I was no longer alone or maybe it was the luck of finding such a useful animal that was something more than food.

That evening, I whittled on my front porch. It was a coat of arms with a wolf in the center howling at the moon. It was a self-portrait. The howling wolf screaming in the agony of losing his father and best friend during the night of a full moon. The horse grazed on the grass, staying close to me.

"It seems you need a name. What do you think?"

He lifted his head, one eye on me. I took that as a yes.

I thought for a long moment before the name popped into my head. "Amit. Yes. That's a good name." I stroked his mane and decided to leave him free to roam. An animal should not be tied up unless a wolf man was on the loose. Yes, during the full moon I'd bring him inside and tomorrow start building a stable for him, a castle of his own.

chapter 3

I had grown habitual in my tasks as I ladled my bowl of stew and peered out the window at the trees. But this morning a new sight — Amit. My companion. He hadn't run off. I felt myself smiling again for the second time within twenty-four hours.

I strapped the leather sack of quivers over my back and grabbed my bow. It was hunting day. Amit watched as I marched into the woods. He didn't follow as if he knew I didn't need the help. My senses were keen and my aim on target.

The only well-worn path on the property led to the stream. Hunting day, I followed my sense of smell and hearing to lead me to prey. My bow steady, I followed a brown rabbit with my eye. His head lifted towards me as though he could see me, but he didn't move. His nose twitched then in a moment he jumped but I'd countered and aimed my arrow slightly to the left. It dug into his side and he dropped.

"I'm sorry little rabbit," I said as I picked him off the forest floor and broke his tiny neck to put him out of his pain. "Don't worry, little guy, you will not be wasted."

Leaves crunched quietly behind me. I turned, readied the bow and shot, catching a white-tailed deer. A young buck by the weight of his steps on the leaves. I didn't kill does as a moral thing. They could be pregnant, occasionally fawns too young to breed and young bucks. My reflexes were quick, quicker than the animals of the forest. I was the top of the food chain. The deer ran with the bow in its side.

Grabbing the rabbit, I followed the buck's steps through the dense forest until it finally collapsed. His brown eyes staring at me in pain as I gently stroked its fur before breaking its neck. "Thank you for your contribution."

Human breathing carried on the wind stopped me in mid-motion as I was about to claim my buck. Straightening, I listened. It was most definitely human and shallow, but close. I shut my eyes, allowing my senses to paint a picture. *Lub dub, lub dub.* Its heartbeat fainter than its breath. Female and young judging by its pheromones.

My keen senses guided me further into the woods. Lying face down in the leaf clutter and dirt was a woman. Her skin red and long hair black, clothed in a buckskin dress — a native I guessed. I knelt next to her and lifted the hair from her neck, brushing it to her back. Her straight nose and high cheek bone enamored me. She was beautiful and unconscious.

I thought of my game. My shoulders broad and my muscles strong, it would still be impossible to bring her back on one shoulder, my buck on the other, and the rabbit in my hand. Faced with the dilemma, I chose to leave my buck for the nocturnal predators and fit her snuggly on a shoulder, holding her with my hand and taking my rabbit with the other.

It would be enough for a couple days if I stretched it and I had plenty of apples, although they would do little to feed my voracious appetite. My first priority was the young woman. I couldn't imagine what she was doing here. It was obvious to me Amit was hers or her transportation. *What caused him to throw her? Why was she travelling alone to begin with?* Many questions filled my mind.

I laid her on my bed as it was the only one in my gigantic home. Stacks of pelts made it soft. With a buckskin cloth I washed the dirt from her face, neck, arms, and legs then lifted her head and brought water from a ladle to her mouth. The water drained down her throat. I laid her down and turned her head to the side, pulled a pelt over her for warmth and stoked a fire in the room. From a chair across the bed I rested in case she awoke. I didn't want her frightened. A smile edging the corners of my lips as I fell asleep.

Over the next few days she slept and I didn't go far, catching game close to my home. I started building a stable for Amit. It would be past the full moon by the time it was ready, but I had enough rooms in the house to accommodate him through one full moon.

All the while, she slept on my bed, her slight body resting on the pelts, the fire stoked, keeping her warm at night as fall was quickly approaching.

I howled as my body transformed into a wolf. It was the shame I carried, making sure to shift far from my home to keep Amit and the young native woman safe. Gray fur replaced the hair on my face and body, my nose elongated into a snout, my feet and hands turned into paws. Tingles rushed through my body with the change. It had to be a family curse. Something a witch did. *Why hadn't my father ever warned me?*

The following morning, I awoke on my spot on the leafy ground outside my home. I always returned there no matter how far I went to change or traveled as a wolf. They say a dog always finds its way home: that was truer than people knew.

I squinted my eyes at the bright morning sun. Movement from the corner of my eye forced me to turn my head. On the steps to my home, the young native woman sat, a pelt over her shoulders to stave off the cold air.

chapter 4

er almond eyes stared at me, confusion tugging at the corners of her lips and wrinkling her nose. I was speechless as I scrambled to my feet, covering my genitalia.

She lifted her head, her eyes fixed on mine as if she was trying to tell me something.

"I don't usually sleep outside. It was a rough night," I stammered as my cheeks reddened in shame.

Her nose crinkled more and her eyes narrowed as she tossed the blanket around her towards me, stood, turned on her heel and walked back into the house.

I wrapped the fur around my waist and entered after her, quickly walking past her to my bedroom. One leg into my usual buckskins, I changed my mind. Today was a beautiful day. She was awake. I had company for as long as she would stay so I pulled on a pair of trousers I'd picked up on a trade and a buttoned shirt. I'd look presentable for her.

I felt along my chin, deciding my unruly beard needed a trim. I couldn't imagine what was stuck in it from my night as a wolf. Grabbing the only mirror in the house, I glanced at my chin; twigs, leaves but, thankfully, no blood. The comb stuck as I ran it through and decided I would trim and comb after.

Feeling better about my appearance, but still embarrassed for my earlier actions, I entered the kitchen. She was perched at the table. A smile tugging at her lips. I supposed this was a very precarious situation for her too but she seemed to take it well. She didn't run, throw things at me, threaten me, nor did she appear the least bit scared.

"I'm Owyn. I found you not far from my house, just other there," I pointed as I rambled. "I uh… what… what is your name?" I wasn't sure how to start the conversation and less sure I'd said anything right.

She cocked her head to the side then stood and walked to the window. Glancing over her shoulder she pointed out the window into the sky. I didn't understand.

I raked a hand through the thick, curly, sun-bleached mop on my head. "It's a beautiful day," I said, watching the birds pick at the food in the homemade bird feeders that hung from my porch.

She bit her bottom lip and pointed again then pointed at herself.

"You want to go outside. I can take you for a ride to the apple grove and the stream."

A scowl covered her face as she pointed again to herself than outside towards the sky. At this point I didn't get it. *Was she mute? Was it the lingering effects of being thrown from Amit? Maybe she didn't want to talk to the guy who slept outside on the grass.*

"I'm sorry. You must be hungry," I changed the subject. Grabbing a bowl, I emptied a ladle full of rabbit stew into it and poured a glass of water.

I set them on the table. "This is all I have, but I will cook a meal fit for a queen for dinner." I wanted to assure her I wasn't a complete hermit with no social graces. It had been years, but my father trained me well. Company always received the best. In this case, such beautiful company deserved all I could give.

She came to me, pressed her hand against mine and pointed outside again then to herself. She didn't give up.

She did it again and it finally dawned on me. "You're Sky," I blurted.

A smile erupted on her face as she nodded in delight. Her dark almond eyes twinkling.

I felt really stupid at this point but she didn't seem to mind as she sat down and ate heartily every bit of rabbit stew in her bowl, then asked for seconds by lifting her bowl and pointing to the stove.

All I had in the house was rabbit and it was nearly finished. To make a meal fit for a queen I had to go hunting. She eyed me while I geared up, strapping my bow to my back. I met her curious gaze. "I have to hunt. I'll return and we'll feast."

My long-leggedstride took me to the quickly to the door. I opened it and glanced over my shoulder at her, as if to make sure she was real. She smiled. The rays of the sun caught her black hair. It shined like fine silk. I strode down the porch and down the steps. My sensitive hearing didn't miss her soft steps as she strolled after me. My ears building a picture as her feet made the slightest crunch on the dry grass.

Amit ran around the corner of the house and past me. So much for spoiling the animal. He made it clear who he belonged to when he stopped in front of her. I turned on my heel. Her arms out for him. He didn't hesitate to nuzzle her hands and chest.

It was as if, somehow, they were communicating on a level even my keen senses couldn't hear. He was obviously her horse and I didn't hesitate to think he found me in order to save her. I rested against a beam of the long, wide porch and watched.

She climbed onto his back as if it was the most natural thing and they trotted towards me. A large smile beaming across her face and in her dark eyes. Amit halted when they reached me.

"You want to go hunting?" I asked, without a response. I didn't expect one. The reunion between the two was all the response I needed. It probably wasn't hunting she wanted but to feel the wind in her hair and stretch her legs. After all, she'd been sleeping for days.

"Fine, let's go." I didn't plan on them hunting with me but would take them to the stream and apple orchard.

Birds twitted in the treetops, rustling the leaves, and squirrels jumped and scurried up their trunks. The sounds of the forest and Amit's trotting filled my ears as we walked into the forest. As we approached the stream, its flowing water pushed at stones beneath its surface adding to the melody.

Sky stirred things in me that I'd forgotten; companionship, friendship, and the fact that I wasn't alone in the world. Joy filled my heart and added pep to my steps as we separated when we reached the stream. Amit continued trotting upstream while I went in the other direction, following another sound my ears picked up on — a deer. By the weight of its footfalls, a young buck.

chapter 5

The three-point buck no match for the speed of my reflexes, he went down. I flung him over my shoulder and headed back towards the stream. My senses attuned, they searched for Sky and Amit's scent. Immediately, I found Amit's, but not hers. My guts twisted into a ball as I reached out with all my feelers and came up empty.

Running towards Amit, I reached him on the side of the stream, alone and unharmed. He lifted his head and eyed me as I approached him. If didn't know better, I'd say he wore a look of surprise as his eyes studied mine. "Where is she?" I asked him without a response.

My back to the stream, I heard the sound of dribbling water before I saw. I jumped full circle, ready to take on whatever was in the stream. I didn't expect what I found.

Sky's wet head above the water. The sun shining on her velvet black hair. She turned and lifted up when she spotted me then sunk back into the water. Her eyes wide in surprise.

Red filled my cheeks as I stumbled over my words. "I uh…" It took my mind a minute to register maybe she didn't need saving, instead wanted me to turn around so I wouldn't see her nakedness. "I'm turning around."

You idiot! my mind mocked. *First, she finds you sleeping on the grass outside. What kind of person does that? Next, you gawk at her while she's bathing. What is wrong with you?* The thoughts rumbled through my head as I tried hard to ignore them.

I listened as she stepped out of the water and gasped when I saw her dress propped on a bush in front of me. My mind so filled with worry and anxiety creeping in my gut I hadn't noticed it before. I grabbed it and put my hand behind my back.

The crunch of rocks along the streambed and mush of the grass warmed my senses as she moved towards me. The dress released from my hand and her breathing filled my ears. A sweet aroma drifted towards my nostrils as I took her in. My mind building a mental picture of her beauty.

A gentle touch on my back told me it was OK to turn around. The straight edge of her chin, the rise of her cheek bones as her lips lifted in a partial smile, and her vibrant brown eyes, I completely forgot about the deer on my wide shoulder and the complete moron I must seem to her. She lifted a hand and pressed it against the deer and shut her eyes as if praying over the deer or giving it last rights.

In that moment, the world froze, and I considered how this beautiful woman hadn't woken fearful. Most anyone else would be scared, maybe think I meant to harm them, but not her. She trusted me, of all people: me. I was half wild animal and much larger than her, yet she didn't shrink beside me in alarm.

Her head held high, when she opened her eyes they met mine as her hand lowered from the deer, brushing over mine. Warmth from her touch worked its way through my extremities.

She nodded at Amit and he trotted to her side and began the journey home. I followed behind them, after a moment. My eyes unable to look away from her long legs. Their toned muscles moving with the rhythm of her steps. It was a nice view and one I couldn't peel my eyes away from until we reached the house and she turned to face me.

My cheeks felt on fire this time, as if caught in a lie or stealing. Immediately, I swept my eyes to her face. She responded with a tilt of her head, her dark hair falling over her cheek.

That night, we feasted on venison and homemade apples in brown sugar and cinnamon. Over the next month, we grew closer. She helped around the house and my feelings for her developed into something I hadn't felt in a while but couldn't pinpoint whether it was having company, all my loneliness washed away, or if it was something more.

Her presence made me feel normal and forget the monster lurking inside me as I went to bed the night of the full moon and awoke with my limbs covered in fur. Still mostly human, urgency pressed me out of the house and as far as I could run before the wolf completely took over. In a rush to not get caught, as that would be worse than embarrassment. I didn't want her of all people to know what I was. Surely it would send her and Amit away.

Owyn, a sweet voice called through the trees. The wolf in me halting, sniffing the air, the ground in search of its origin. At that moment, even as a wolf I was human.

Catching the sweet, familiar aroma, my legs took over and carried me back to the house. Its three stories looming into the sky. Coming up from the backside, I trotted around it and found Sky perched on a wooden chair on the front porch.

Her movements cautious, she lifted from the chair and padded towards me. My wolf self didn't move, as if she had some power over me. *Owyn, you didn't have to hide who you are.*

Her words a melody in my head. *How was it possible she could reach my wolf brain?*

My people, we speak to all life in the forest. The trees, the animals, the birds, and plants. She reached my stationary body and knelt, running a hand along my jaw. *You are kind and I owe you my life. Don't be afraid of who you are.*

Who am I? I thought and answered my own thought, *a wild animal.*

No, you're not wild. Her hand moved to the top of my head. Her touch soothing.

She was reading my mind as I stood there in the chilly air as a wolf and all I could think to ask was: *Who are your people?*

She averted her gaze from me and stared at the ground beside my feet. *They have scattered. Our village was raided by true monsters. The forest warned us and that's how I and the horse you call Amit ended up here.*

The shock wearing off that we could communicate brain to brain as the reality of her words clutched me. True monsters. I knew those monsters. *Long faces, sharp jagged teeth, claws instead of hands.*

She nodded, lifting her gaze from the ground, meeting mine. *We are a gentle people, orators of nature.*

All I could think of was helping her people, bringing them here where I could give them safety. I could use my extra senses to track them. *Where is your village?*

It's a day and a half's journey and probably destroyed, but I will take you there at first light. She rested her head against my face. *Please, go, hunt. Let the wolf in you run without feeling shame.*

She stood then and turned on her heel, walking up the steps to the porch, then paused and glanced over her shoulder *Thank you, Owyn.* Her voice music in my head. Like a heavy weight had dropped from my shoulders, I felt freer than I ever had as I ran towards the trees.

I remember nothing more of that night. I awoke in the morning buck naked on the crusty, brittle, autumn grass. Our conversation fuzzy like a dream.

chapter 6

A pair of buckskin pants and a shirt lay over the back of one of the porch chairs. A smile swept my face as I pushed one leg then another through the pants and pulled the shirt over my head. The dream fuzzy but alive. I wondered if she'd seen me as a wolf the night she woke and that's why she hadn't feared me. A question I would keep pondering, as I wasn't about to ask and embarrass myself all over again.

I opened the door to see Sky at the stove, the buckskin dress snug around her figure. Her back to me, she glanced over her shoulder hearing the door, me, or both, then grabbed a bowl, ladled stew into it and set it on the table in front of me.

I pulled out a chair and sat, letting her take care of me how I'd taken care of her. Lifting a spoon of stew toward my mouth I paused as she took a seat across from me. Her long hair falling over her shoulder and an expectant expression with her hands folded beneath her chin and her eyes meeting mine. By her actions I guessed our conversation had happened but still I had to ask. "Last night, that was real, wasn't it?"

She nodded.

That was all I needed. As I ate, I talked out my plan with her using her body language to guide me.

We'd pack plenty of apples, venison jerky, and water, load it on Amit along with plenty of furs to keep us warm, and I didn't say it but to keep any survivors, if there were any, toasty as well. She'd ride Amit and I'd walk. My stride long and legs quick, I could keep pace and there wouldn't be room for both of us and gear on Amit. She would lead and I'd keep my senses peeled. Other than trading, I hadn't traveled beyond the land I'd claimed.

I didn't know exactly what we'd do or what I'd do when we got there, or even what I expected to find. I hoped nothing, hoped everyone would be gone. But I braced for death the closer we got. When the sun lowered in the sky and the woods grew dark, we stopped for the night.

I got a fire started while she laid out the bear pelt. It was soft, and with the fire we were snug. She stacked the other pelts beside us as we feasted on jerky and apples. She twisted her mouth as she gnawed at the jerky.

Grabbing a stick, she drew in the sand. I admired the profile of her face and jawline. Lost in her exquisiteness, I didn't notice when she finished until she turned her head. Her eyes narrowed, she sighed deeply as if trying to tell me something.

She tapped the stick and I glanced at the picture she'd drawn of plants, wheat, corn, pears, peaches, and plums. The detail caught me before its meaning.

When it became clear what she meant I nearly blurted, "There're gardens?"

She nodded, then mimicked picking them up and carrying them. "We can take some and grow gardens at…" I hadn't named my house. It was that moment I decided it was deserving of a name, besides 'home'. "… Wolf Manor."

Her lovely full lips curled into a smile. Yes, we'd learned to communicate without actual words. That didn't make the conversation in my wolf form less important. The idea she could communicate with me as a wolf gave me hope. The fact I didn't attack and harm her gave me more hope. Maybe, I had more control than I thought as a wolf, or wasn't the monster I considered myself to be.

She moved closer to me, her scent intoxicating as she drew Wolf Manor. The more I thought about the name, the more perfect it felt. Behind the house was an empty field as I'd used the trees to build. She drew lines in various directions and labeled them. Along the stream she drew trees and labeled them.

In her mind she planned it all out and in the dirt in front of me was her gardening plan. I'd taken what nature gave me and never complained. I took this as a hint she was tired of my meat and apple diet. She wanted more variety.

A chill fell over us and I reached around behind her and grabbed a pelt, pulling it over her shoulders. She clutched it together in the front. "You can plant all you want," I said, welcoming the idea of diversifying our diet. I loved the thought of "our" even more.

Another thought occurred to me. If she planned on building a garden, then she planned on staying at least long enough to harvest. She laid her head against my shoulder. I hadn't felt human contact in so long. I didn't want the moment to end.

Once she was asleep, I lowered her across the bear pelt and lay beside her, pulling the last pelt over us. It would get colder and the fire would die. Our body heat inside the pelt would keep us warm until morning.

The sweet scent of her body and hair lulled me to sleep.

The sun streamed through the trees, begging me to awake. Upon opening my eyes, Sky was turned towards me, her eyes studying my face. She smiled then pushed a long, wild curl off my cheek. That tender moment only lasted a short moment before she stood and tossed me an apple from the leather pouch on Amit's back.

Anxiety roiled in my gut with each step. The fact I didn't know what we'd find ate at me, frightened me, but Sky held strong as if she knew a secret I didn't. I couldn't tell if she shared my fears as Amit trotted ahead of me. By the time the sun was at its highest point in the sky, Amit halted.

Sky dismounted and walked ahead through trees. I followed until we reached the edge of the low mountain, below us a small village, semi-permanent wood structures with thatched roofs surrounded by woods. The odor of death lingered in the air. She took my hand and brought our entwined hands forward in the direction of the little village.

"You stay here with Amit. I'll go down," I said. The trail down was rocky, and I feared her losing her footing, but not as much as I feared what I'd find inside the makeshift homes. Carnage wasn't something I wanted her to see.

I considered how much easier it would be to trek down the mountain as wolf but dispelled that idea quickly as I didn't have control and would likely forget what I was doing there. No, I had to go as a human. The rocks unsteady under my feet as I slowly stepped over them, following the trail. The stench of death stronger the closer I got.

When I reached the bottom, I glanced upwards. I'd come a good thirty feet and Sky was nowhere to be seen which to me meant she'd gone back to Amit and was waiting like I'd asked. It was some comfort knowing she wasn't waiting at the ledge for me.

I paused, opened my senses, and listened for any signs of life or death, then shifted my attention to Sky. I didn't want to be wrong and wouldn't be able to live with myself if something were to happen to her. I'd lost too much already. The steady beat of her heart pounded in my ears, telling me she was calm and in no danger.

In the village, no sounds of breathing, shallow or not, no patter of footsteps, a faint smell of sweat lingered in the air as I drew nearer the village, but it was faint, from sometime in the near past, or maybe it was me, I thought as I wrinkled my nose. There were no signs of life whatsoever.

Pushing aside the buckskin door on the first wood structure, I reached inside. It was empty. As if whoever was there had completely vacated. I remembered she told me the forest warned them. Going from one home to the next, all were near bare. *If they had enough time to vacate with all their belongings why wouldn't they stay together?*

I asked myself that question as I stood in the middle of the little village. The death I smelled wasn't theirs. It was the stench the demons left behind. The same I smelled in St. Augustine the night I lost my father and best friend. Kneeling on one knee, I placed my palm against the ground, closed my eyes and allowed my senses to paint the picture.

Horses and people scattered, heading every direction. Little ones cried, unsure what was happening. The demons came through soon after, leaving their stench on everything as they invaded the small village, upset it was vacant. I pointed my nose upward and sniffed. South, they turned around and headed south.

Her people were a simple people. They didn't have much, making it so easy for them to leave in such a hurry. A sweet scent assailed my nostrils as they welcomed it over the stench I wanted to forget. I opened my eyes and tilted my head. A few feet from me stood a little girl. Her large brown eyes wide inside her chubby face.

"Hi," I said as I offered my hand, slowly standing so as not to alarm her.

She blinked but didn't run.

"I can help you. Do you know Sky?"

Her eyes beamed recognition with the name and she lifted her arm as if extending a hand for me. Leaves rustled in the woods. Immediately, I pinpointed the direction and swung myself in front of the girl to protect her. Forgetting to use my extra senses. I was ready to devour whatever was in the woods.

chapter 7

When Sky appeared, I relaxed and felt stupid I hadn't immediately known it was her. It was the dread in my gut that momentarily blinded my senses. The little girl pressed her hands against the back of my legs and peered out.

Sky's face immediately lit up as she dropped to her knees and welcomed the child who scurried into her arms.

I stood, perplexed. How did this girl, no more than about three, maybe four, survive so long? It had been over a month. And where were her parents? As if this girl was the entire reason we came, Sky turned and headed into the woods, a buckskin bag flapping against her thigh as she walked.

My first reaction was alarm that she walked away from me. That reaction was followed by sadness and rejection. *Had I done something wrong?* My chest tightened in sorrow. "Wait," I called. "This girl hasn't survived on her own. She's too young. Where are her parents?"

Sky didn't wait as she kept going until we came to another clearing filled with gardens flowing with overgrown vegetables. Some had been picked open by birds and other herbivores. Sky set the girl down and glanced over her shoulder at me then pointed.

I followed her movements as she walked into the garden, pulling seeds out of the vegetables and stuffing them into the leather pouch hanging against her thigh. When I didn't immediately follow her, she pointed into the woods.

My chest loosened as I felt relief. She wasn't upset at all, probably overwhelmed herself with emotions at finding the girl. Sky propped a hand on her hip, her eyes fixed to mine as she glared and pointed.

After over a month with her, I knew what she wanted and, judging by her actions, needed to jump out of my relief- gaze, which I imagined looked fairly stupid, and get to it. In the forest was more. The girl scampered to Sky's side as I entered the woods.

They weren't ordinary woods but filled with fruit trees; peaches and plums and the other fruit from her drawing. Remnants of fruit were scattered on the ground. Collecting a few of each, my hands becoming a stinky mess, I brought them back to Sky.

She stuck her hands into the fruit, collecting the seeds. How would she remember which seed belonged to which plant? *Was this something she was taught?*

The little girl held tight to Sky's hand as we followed her out of the garden, through the woods, up the hill to where Amit stood waiting for us. She lifted the girl onto Amit's back then climbed up behind her. After all, we couldn't leave the child.

We stopped for the night when the sun went down. I had so many questions for her and I didn't doubt I could track most, if not all, paths the villagers took. The only way for me to hold a conversation with her was to change into a wolf and with the little girl around I didn't think that was the best choice. I didn't want to scare her, yet she hadn't spoken, so maybe she was like Sky.

I kept my questions to myself for the time being as we settled onto the bear pelt. The little girl falling asleep, her head in Sky's lap, soon after eating. Fine, dark hair trailed over the girl's tiny cheeks and her chest rose and fell with each breath. Small, chubby fingers clutched the bearskin.

We arrived at Wolf Manor the following night. The child asleep in Sky's arms, her head tilted to the side. I lifted her off Amit's back.

Her small body fell against mine and she rested her head on my shoulder. I carried her inside the house and laid her on my bed. A goofy smile in my face with all the joy filling my heart that had been empty so long.

Sky entered the house soon after and stood in the doorway of the room, her arms loose around her chest as she smiled fondly. Meeting her at the door, I took her hand and guided her into the great room. "I'm going to change, become a wolf, and I need you to tell me what happened, answer my questions."

She nodded confirmation and turned as I stripped and allowed my wolf out. I'd never done it inside the house and felt awkward as fur sprung from my extremities, my nose elongated into a snout, and my back prickled as I took on the form of the wolf. I hoped I'd remember everything I'd repeated in my mind the past thirty-six hours.

Owyn, she called as my paws padded the wooden floor and I sat on my haunches in front of her.

The thoughts rolled off my brain. *You knew she was there?*

Yes, I sensed her fear when we got close enough. Her parents didn't make it, but she was safely hidden away. The forest protected her, took care of her.

Is she one of your people?

Yes. Her name is Blossom, as she was born during the time when blossoms were everywhere. She hasn't been alone long. I don't know how her parents died, only that they did. She has no one but us.

She knelt, placing her hands on her legs.

Us. That had a nice ring to it. I said again in my mind for good measure, *Us. Agree. She needs us. I can use my senses to track. We can bring them all here. There's plenty of room.*

There's no need. They will find me, the forest and the animals carry the message.

I didn't know what that meant. It would be snowing and ice-cold soon. No one should travel in such harsh weather. She was filled with surprises, so I didn't ask. The door would be open when they got here.

She placed a hand on my face. *What about you?*

Me. I had no one. *They're dead. Others like you.*

There wasn't anyone like me. My father was a wolf man as I

learned on his final day, but not like me. He was more human than wolf.

She planted the seed in my head that night. Who would know about my father, be like my father? *Did I have other family?* My mother died giving birth to me. I'd never known her. It was my father and I as long as I remembered until that horrific night. *Where did my family come from?*

chapter 8

Blossom, unlike Sky, was very talkative. She asked all types of questions and bounced from the time the sun woke up until it went to bed. Her energy and inquisitiveness were contagious.

I left Sky and Blossom at Wolf Manor, as winter was quickly approaching and we needed more supplies to pull through it. I made sure to show Sky the basement. It was safely hidden, but would be there if they needed it for safety. The demons had come as close as a day and a half's journey. That was too close for my comfort. I hesitated to leave them, but they needed more than meat and apples.

Amit and I arrived in the closest trading village. It consisted of a collection of a few buildings, including a lodge, church, trade post, and a few homes. Most of the homes were spread out along the river. Large, towering trees with vibrant red, gold, and yellow leaves surrounded the small but growing area. More people had settled since I'd visited last.

The collection of skins, furs, and fresh apples bought cloth to make new dresses for Sky and Blossom, flour, plenty of dried fruit, a basket of dried herbs for Sky, and seeds. She'd salvaged as many as she could from her village, but I wasn't sure that would be enough. If we were expecting more people we'd need food and a variety to plant in the spring after the last frost.

I took a room for the night at the lodge. I would head home at first light. While others laughed and chattered, gathering around the many wooden barrel tables spread throughout the lodge tavern, I sat alone at the bar. I'd tried my own hand at making ale, however, I learned I should stick to carpentry. The ale here had a sweet, woodsy taste. It wasn't the best but was better than my attempt.

A young man with dark hair falling over his shoulders and a long black leather coat sat down on the empty barstool next to me. I didn't pay much attention to him at first, other than a quick glance acknowledging his presence.

"Not horrible," the young man said wiping his hand across his face after a swig of the ale. He didn't look older than I was myself when I ran from St. Augustine that horrible night of the attack. The thought still brought shivers coursing up my spine.

"I've had worse," I responded.

The man tilted his head, his golden eyes meeting mine. "Lars."

"Owyn." I offered my hand and he accepted in a quick shake. His skin unusually cool to the touch. I averted my gaze to the candlelight bouncing off the mirror behind the bar.

After several minutes of silence, Lars broke it. I felt his gaze travel my profile, head to toe, pausing for a beat. "You are quiet. All these people and you sit by yourself." It was more a question than a statement.

It wasn't the fact that I had nothing to talk about as much as I didn't know anyone, which gave me less to talk about, and I'd lived alone many years and now with a mute woman who only spoke when I was in wolf form.

"Can I buy you another?" Lars asked as he waved the bartender over. "I'm passing through, for the night. I don't know anyone either, so thought I'd sit next to the guy by himself."

I gulped the ale, hoping he'd go away, but no such luck. He had a charm about him, but I wasn't much in a mood for socializing.

He started in on a story, to make conversation I assumed. "On my walk here I ran across a bear, six feet tall, burly," he used his hands to show the size of the animal, "and I'm out of arrows. My choice is to run but I know he'll catch me and rip me apart with his teeth. There's a tree only a few steps from me, so I climb it. I end up sleeping over-night in that tree. As the day breaks, I look and see the bear is still there and I'm thinking…" He presses a finger to his temple. "… I'm going to have to stay in the tree. If I climb down, I'm dead. The funniest thing happens. The bear suddenly sniffs the air then gallops away, the ground rumbling beneath him. I think, 'Great. Now I can continue on my way,' and as I climb down the tree, one foot still on the lowest branch, I start to wonder why the bear ran away. Both feet planted on the ground, I see it. On the ridge is the largest wolf I've ever laid eyes on. It's staring at me. I can climb back into the tree, but I'd have the same problem I did with the bear. I don't know what to do. The wolf doesn't move and it doesn't frighten me. Next thing, he turns and runs in the opposite direction like somebody rang the breakfast bell and it's time to go home."

He pauses, his golden eyes searching mine. "You ever seen a wolf like that?" The tone in his voice making it apparent the question had a deeper meaning.

A chill manifested in my gut. If I hadn't known better, I'd think that final comment was aimed directly at me. "Nope."

He glanced away. "You have a good night." He stood and exited up the steps.

The man, more than the story, left me perplexed. Why would anyone wander into the woods without protection and hunting gear? He did look odd in his long leather coat, definitely not fitting into the current crowd as I eyed the patrons in their trousers and buckskins.

Tired from the day and the journey, I gulped the last of the ale and headed up the stairs to the bed waiting for me. I quickly fell into sleep but awoke covered in sweat when the man appeared in my dream. His golden eyes glowing in his finely featured face, dark hair moving as if pushed by wind. His words or warning, 'Go now, before daybreak. They are coming.'

Sitting on the edge of the bed, my chin in my hands, I considered if it was more than a dream. *Was it induced by the ale?* His face was there. I still saw it in my mind, clear as the moment it happened. *Who was coming?*

chapter 9

I spent the rest of the night pacing while I considered my options. I had people to take care of. I didn't want trouble, but who was coming and why would they want anything with me? Leaving and heading home made sense, but could I run again? If danger was approaching, as the dream suggested, and I ran that would be like running out on my father and Horacio and leaving my bride to be again.

No! I chose to stay. If whatever was coming was as frightening as the demons, I could handle it. My father's words when he'd given the knife to me: 'It's made from the bones of demon hunters. One cut with it and they will die.' My father half man, half wolf, was a demon hunter. I'd seen him kill them with a bite. I, like him, was a demon hunter in my wolf form and possibly had the ability to kill them with one bite. The thought of tasting their flesh and black, tar-like blood sickened me. I'd stick to the knife.

If demons were coming I was going to stand up this time and fight, not run like a coward and hide like a weak, scared child. But first, I had to find Lars. The story he told, he knew something.

The lodge served breakfast, lunch, and dinner, strong coffee and stronger ale. I ordered a plate of eggs and waited. Others flowed into the tavern, but not him. I watched him ascend the stairs to a room the previous night. *He'd come to me in my dream, where had he gone?*

I took the steps two at a time and flung the first door open, then the next and the next. I didn't believe people were still in them and if they were, I'd apologize and move on. They were empty. The room next to mine, a folded note was on the small round wooden table next to the bed. It said: *Owyn.*

Opening it, I scanned the writing. *Monastery in St. Augustine Father Bornecke,* and beneath that: *You are one, they are many. Leave now!*

I ruminated for several minutes on the meaning of the note and whether I should leave as Lars so heavily suggested. Hesitating no longer, I packed my goods on

Amit's back and headed home, convincing myself along the ride that I was making the wise decision not the coward decision. Sky and Blossom were waiting for my return and, if they were looking for me, they wouldn't find me there. This may save the people more than making a stand against the demons. If it was the demons.

In the spring, I'd travel to St. Augustine and find Father Bornecke. Maybe he'd have the answers I'd long pushed into the back of my mind. *What are demon hunters? Why did I lose my mother before ever getting to know her? What is special about our bones? Why do I transform into a wolf?*

I stopped for the night, hidden in the trees. I didn't start a fire in case whoever the '*they*' Lars warned

about were near. Wrapping a pelt
tightly around me, I rested my head
on a bundle of leaves on the
ground and stared into the sky.
Stars twinkled through the leaves
still hanging from tree branches.

In my slumber, Lars stole into
my mind again. His golden eyes
shining bright. *It is only safe in your
mind, the queen watches my every move
but she cannot see when I dream walk.
You made the right choice. Protect those
you love and come for us one day when
you are many.*

His face vanished and I woke,
sun breaking through the branches,
his words resonating in my mind:
'*Come for us*' - meaning he was one
of them. But what were they? The
demons, or something else?
Mounting Amit, we rode the rest of

the way to Wolf Manor, arriving in the dark.

Sky greeted me at the door, her face beaming in joy. Voices from inside carried to my ears like music. I entered the great room to find a young couple. Their skin the color of Sky's, long dark silky hair on their heads, and dark eyes. They stopped talking when I entered and stood.

With a stern face the man spoke, "We thank you for your kindness taking in Sky and Blossom. You are a man of strength and generosity. We ask for your permission to stay through the cold months."

I brimmed with joy. It was my pleasure for them to stay. "There's more than enough room, stay as long as you like. I hope you will come to think of Wolf Manor as more than a place of temporary refuge but home."

The man's eyes softened. "Thank you. I am Fire and this is Butterfly," he said, grabbing the hand of the young woman who rose and stood at his side.

chapter 10

Over the winter Butterfly and Fire turned into a great help as we built furniture for the rooms in the house, made bread, clothes, and showed Fire how to whittle. In return, he showed me how to make ale from apples. We made toys for Blossom and the child he and Butterfly were expecting.

Snow covered the ground and cold surrounded the house, but inside was warm and filled with life. Butterfly informed me Sky had never had the ability to speak through her mouth but spoke through her mind stronger than any other. She was their beacon, and others would follow.

Having a stronger mental ability made sense. If she had no ability to speak with her mouth then she needed to speak louder with her mind.

It was the second snow when more appeared. A family of five. The snow reigning above my head, I added to Amit's stable with the help of Fire and our newest male members. The structure sound enough to last the winter. In the spring, we would make it permanent and expand it further.

Sky and I grew even closer, her heart overflowing and mine beaming with joy. My lonely life but a bad dream that seemed a lifetime ago. She taught me to accept the wolf in me, showed me it was a blessing and not a curse. We had long conversations. I told her about my trip to the trading village and Lars.

You must go, learn who you are, she encouraged.

The night of the second full moon of the winter she beckoned me inside after my run, opening the front door for me. I followed her to my room where she encouraged me to change back into human form. I stood before her naked. She didn't look away but sat on the edge of the bed and lifted the pelt on the bed then padded towards me.

Her eyes fixed on mine, she slipped out of her gown, letting it drop to the floor, then took my hands. My eyes delighted in the curves of her body and she stepped out of the pile of gown at her ankles. My hands went to her waist, her skin softer than any pelt. I lowered my head, our lips brushed. Excitement tingled inside me as we kissed, awakening a part of me I'd forgotten.

I picked her up and laid her on the bed where we continued to kiss and explore each other. I'd always been attracted to her, but couldn't imagine a woman as beautiful as her interested in a rugged, bulky man who was part wolf, like me.

That night was the beginning in the next phase of our relationship. Blossom gained a room of her own as Sky took to my bed most nights. Smiles from the others showed their acceptance of our union.

chapter 11

Snow gave way to green leaves and buds and warmer air. It was time for me to return to St. Augustine. I packed all I needed for the trip on Amit's back and begged Sky to stay. She was needed to get the gardens started and plant the trees. This was my journey, and one that could be filled with danger.

My body tightened as Amit's hooves clomped over the solid earth beneath us. Palm trees swayed in the breeze from the bay, pushing over them. People crossed the street in their high-collared shirts and dresses, small children ran behind their parents.

My eyes unwillingly scanned each face searching for Portencia, the bride I'd left behind. It had been so many years, I imagined she'd moved on, found a husband who wasn't a monster and had children. We'd planned a large family. My carpentry skills not only made a decent wage, but we planned a large home of our own.

When I started building Wolf Manor it was our plan my mind kept referring to,except I didn't stop with the modest two story home with a great room, four bedrooms, large kitchen, and parlor. I first dug into the ground, releasing my anger, and fashioned a basement as wide and long as the house itself. Above it, I laid a foundation and built upwards, cutting log after log and shaving beams.

Once the frame was set I thatched a roof to stay dry, eventually I put a proper roof on it. Year after year, sealed in the walls, built a wide staircase that went straight up. Bedrooms lined the second floor and the third floor. At the very top, I made a special room with a large window that looked over hundreds of acres. I designed balconies on each level.

It became far more than I'd ever imagined and large enough to house an army, not at all what Portencia and I had planned. Other than distraction, I never understood my drive to build something so massive but now, with Sky, all the pieces were fitting together.

The monastery wasn't much. Several wood structures with thatched roofs. Azaleas bloomed and palm trees reached to the sky, swaying in the moist afternoon breeze. Sweat soaked my chest and bubbled on my forehead. I hadn't missed the extreme heat and wet air even in the spring months. Monks worked a garden, turning soil and sowing seeds. Children frolicked and played. It wasn't what I expected.

Footsteps behind me alerted my ears someone was close. Turning, a young man in a brown cloak peered at me. His eyes smiling warmly. "Brother Aubin. Welcome!" he said, as I tied Amit.

I'd worked out in my mind what I would say but now the words didn't find their way through my vocal cords.

"Come. You must need a drink after your journey," Brother Aubin offered as his eyes glanced at my appearance.

I followed him inside one of the wooden structures that appeared larger inside than it did outside. Brother Aubin excused himself as I surveyed my surroundings. Several wood tables and chairs covered the floor. I scanned the structure with my carpenter's eyes. Slivers of light shone between the wood slats and the roof appeared to be thatched with palm fronds, judging by the slender leaves folded over and tied onto wooden beams.

I thought of how airy it must be in the one to two months of the year that fell cold. It wasn't the same cold as I experienced at wolf manor, and a warm fire was enough to stave it off in St. Augustine.

The thump of wood on metal as the brother set down a mug drew me out of my thoughts. I found my voice, "Thank you." The cool water was refreshing as it slid down my throat.

The brother's smile dropped. "What is the reason for your visit?"

I swallowed another gulp of the water. "Father Bornecke, is he here?"

His eyebrows knitted as if surprised. "Yes, wait here," he said as he walked away. He didn't ask my business and for a moment a thought that I was expected washed over me, but that was silly.

I was alone with my thoughts. I couldn't sit there, so stood and paced, then paused in front of one of the windows, a large magnolia offering shade from the bright sun stood outside the window. Running a finger along the wood frame, it was rough not shaved.

"Is it not to your liking?" asked a deep voice from behind me.

I whirled around, caught off guard, my eyes met with a man in a brown tunic. He was much taller and wider than the brother. His face buried in a bristly beard of dishwater-blond hair.

"Habit. I'm a carpenter," I answered, feeling guilt over judging the quality of workmanship.

His beard moved as his lips turned upwards in a smile. "Father Bornecke."

"Owyn Nowak," I responded, sucking in a breath as I figured out what to say next.

He nodded. "Let's walk." He cupped his hands behind his back. Exiting through a back door, we stayed under the shade of trees while he talked.

"Your father died many years ago. I am surprised it took you this long. I expected you much sooner."

What was he talking about? Did he know my father? "Expected me?" I asked, my curiosity overwhelming. First Lars, who was one of *us.* Whoever *us* referred to I didn't know. Now the Father *expected* me.

"You sound surprised. Your father didn't tell you," he said, continuing his pace without turning around for me to see his face.

Muddled, confused thoughts spun in circles in my head. "Tell me?"

He slowed his pace to a stop as two children ran past us, giggling. "I'll show you."

I watched the children scamper off. Father Bornecke picked up his pace and opened the door to another building. A taller building with two stories, but still poorly construction.

"The children. Do they live here?" I asked in curiosity, as I'd never set foot in a monastery and had no idea they housed children.

He stepped into the building. "Yes. Unwed mothers commonly leave their children here to be raised."

I mulled that over, still unsure why I needed to come here. I didn't let the idea distract my attention. Inside the long building were rows of pews on either side of the walkway and a pulpit at the end. The same palm tree thatched roof covered the building. It was modest with its wooden walls and lacked any fancy stained glass or frills.

I guessed my idea of a monastery was a grand structure like those of the wealthy churches, but monks lived simple lives.

The door closed behind us and it became very dark. The only light from a couple small, rectangular windows and candles. He continued past the pulpit, which again was very modest, nothing but a wooden case with an open bible. Behind the pulpit was another door, and a corridor that went to the second level.

He took one of the candles in a brass holder as he guided me to the second level. The steps creaked under our weight. At the top was another door. He drew a key from his pocket and unlocked it. It moaned and complained as he slid it open. Wooden crates spread across the floor and dust tickled my nose, making me sneeze.

He shuffled through the crates and pulled one off the ground, setting in on top of another. He lifted his head then and met my gaze. "This is a storage room. When your father died he had possession of items that can be dangerous in the wrong hands." He patted the top of the crate. "These are your father's belongings. Now they are yours."

His face stern, he stepped away from the crate and towards the door.

"Wait, I… uh… didn't come here for his things but answers." I didn't know if I should mention Lars and the cryptic message and his visits to my dreams.

He pointed. "They're in the crate."

"No, my dad he was…" Then I remembered the bone knife and pulled it from my belt and held it in the dim light streaming from the small window.

Father Bornecke cleared his throat. "Lobos de Fuego." His voice edgy and distant.

The word lobos rang a bell as my mind journeyed to the night of my father's death. The demon said, 'We aren't afraid of you lobo'. They called me lobo and fuego meant fire. I knew that much. Wolves of fire — it clicked. The knife made of bone — wolf man bone — burned inside the demons, killing them.

"In that crate are your answers. I'll return." He left the door open and I listened as his footfalls descended the squeaky staircase.

Whatever it was, he wasn't about to tell me without me taking a journey through the crate. I opened the lid, setting in on top of another crate and stared at its contents. A moldy leather book, another weapon of bone — a sword.

I lifted the book, blowing off the dust. A silver wolf face sketched in detail was on the cover.

Inside were sketches of wolf men. I had to turn the book sideways, as that's how they were drawn. They were like my father; human bodies with wolf faces and large paws on their hands and feet. The next page: a woman holding what appeared to be a baby but with a wolf's head.

I flipped to the next page and gasped, the book falling from my hands, my breath stuck in my throat. The face on it washing my brain in a storm of memories of the demons. Catching my breath, I collected the book and stared at the long, oval face, pointy ears, filled black circles for eyes, and jagged fangs protruding from thin lips. The demons.

Pictures filled the book. Wind, uprising ocean waves, tumbling buildings, and humans with outstretched arms as if they were responsible, battles and death. My mind didn't want to understand what the book was telling me. I'd avoided it many years. I already knew. I lived it every full moon, yet I'd distanced myself, hid myself from the world.

The heat in the room almost unbearable, I wiped my brow with my sleeve as it was the only dry part of my shirt. The rest drenched in sweat. Laying the book in the crate I lifted the sword fashioned from bone and ran my palm along the bottom of the smooth blade. My father was part of a secret society that sought out and killed demons.

chapter 12

As if a key unlocked a door in my brain, a flood of memories opened it and washed over me, taking me back in time to that horrible night so many years ago.

The moonlight on my furry back and sorrow heavy in my heart, I stared at my sleeping bride-to-be. My mind a cluster of sorrow and pity, I almost missed the shadows moving on her from the corner of her room. Darkness swept over her.

Pure black rage hijacked my wolf body as the dark figures moved closer to her. Their oblong heads and jagged teeth reflected in the moonlight. I crashed through the window, glass falling over me and shattering further on the ground as my paws landed between her and the creatures. Hideous or not, they couldn't have her.

A snarl rose in my throat, erupting from my mouth. The demons didn't back away, smirks on their faces, and that's when I saw the blood bathing the sheet beneath Portencia. Grief and revulsion thundered to my extremities as I leaped toward the demon closest to myself and ripped his throat out, spitting his leathery flesh on the floor.

The other took that moment of his comrade's death and fled into the night. My heart and instinct belonged with my darling bride as I trotted to her side, lifting my paws over the side of the bed and glancing into her glassy blue eyes. She was dead. Tears rolled over my snout and dropped onto her face.

In my own pity, I was ready to leave her, now she was taken, everything dear to me was taken within moments. The emotions I felt indefinable, and they churned inside me. I wanted nothing more than to rip the throats and black hearts out of each and every demon.

My father's words echoing strong in my head: 'You must kill Horacio or he will become one of them'. A knot the size of a ball formed in my throat as the thought of stabbing Portencia now weighed heavy in my heart. *Did I need to?*

Horacio was still alive. Portencia was not.

I raised a heavy paw to her throat and pressed gently, searching for a pulse. A faint thump against the pads of my paw told me she was alive, but barely. Her blank stare hadn't changed, as if her brain was completely gone. As past emotions bubbled inside my gut, one overwhelmed the others. I was ready to fight for Portencia and wasn't the coward I thought myself to be.

I didn't have the knife. I'd left it, forgotten it, as grief carried me away from my father and Horacio. Glancing over my shoulder, the demon smoldered in a pile of ashes on the wooden floor. The only way I had to kill her was with my teeth. To pull her throat as I had his. I couldn't bring myself to do it. Stepping away from the bed, I bolted through the shattered window.

Guilt, hate, and revenge like I'd never felt guided me as I followed the repulsive stench of death, making them easy to track. Every sense in my body acute, my legs quick as my paws pounded the earth. Shrouded in darkness, I ran through the trees with agility, my nose leading me into the dense woods.

My one-track mind knocked off course when someone hurdled themselves in my path, a sword encircled in radiant blue flames held in the palms of their hands parallel to their chest. A hood covering their head. I skidded to a halt, nearly knocking them over from momentum. My fight wasn't with this person but the demons who stole everyone I loved.

The person's frame slender and tall even in the cloak, I recognized it was a man. He dropped the hood of his cloak, revealing handsome, chiseled features and eyes so bright they blazed in the darkness, cutting through the night.

I recognized him as the man from the alley. One of the sworded slayers who killed the demons.

"You must stop. This isn't yet your battle," he demanded, his expression tight and meaningful.

No words formed in my wolf mouth, only thoughts and confusion. The muddle of emotions bursting inside me simmered and a sense of calm enveloped me like a warm blanket.

Two more people strode from the woods. The dark-skinned woman from the alley, her eyes a glow of emerald and the young man, tufts of thick, dark hair moving freely in the breeze. An orange glow cascaded from his form to mine. The source of the harmony that faded all the bad memories that coursed in me only moments earlier.

The man in blue raised the sword over his back into a sheath. His expression grave and expressive. "I am a seer and we are Slayers. It is our job to hunt and kill the Bloodseekers. You are one and they are many. You are needed to build your army. It will already be happening when this memory is revealed and must be kept secret. No one, including the next generation of Slayers, should know you exist. You will not remember all that has happened since the alley until the time is right."

He stuffed his hand in his pocket and knelt. His face even with mine. Bringing his hand between us he uncurled his fingers, revealing my bone knife. "You will be much older and wiser. Go, leave St. Augustine."

I took the knife in my mouth. My mind became a blank slate as I ran from the woods, my last memory watching Portencia sleep. The Slayer's words buzzed in my head and hung on the phrase: 'It will already be happening'. It had to mean Sky and the other Orators. They were key in whatever battle I was born into but there was a deeper meaning behind it, one I didn't yet understand.

A creak from the steps alerted me that Father Bornecke had returned. I lifted my eyes from the sword to the doorway. A lit candle in his hand, the light bounced against his rugged features. He leaned against a crate. "A sword of fire."

I wanted answers not more treasures. "What can you tell me about this?"

"It is a sword, like your knife, carved from the bone of the first demon hunter." His words grim and face solemn.

I stood, placed the sword into the crate and pushed my arm between us, forcing the change. Gray fur sprang from my arm, my hand took on the form of a wolf.

"This!" I stated firmly, while attempting to hold the partial change.

His expression didn't change as he opened his mouth to speak. "It isn't a short story. Sit."

Not feeling like sitting, I did anyways, not caring that I was drenched from sweating.

He collected the book from the crate and held it against his legs. "Legend says centuries ago a sorceress created monsters with a spell that kept her eternally young. They aren't demons as you might call them, but humans who she forced into servitude for her gain. Ironically, it is also the blood of humans that sustains her youth and the monsters she made — Bloodseekers."

chapter 13

Father Bornecke turned a few pages in the book and flipped it around, displaying the ugly face of the creature I called a demon. It was no demon but a Bloodseeker, created by human hands and magic. The same name the blue Slayer called it — Bloodseeker. He then flipped to the first page and sat on a crate closer to me.

Pointing to the first wolf man and gliding his finger over the page as he told the story. A child was born, strong as Samson with the speed and senses of a wolf. He became a ferocious warrior who many claimed ripped his enemies apart with his sharp wolf teeth. This man had three sons, all of them from different mothers as they died in childbirth. Each son with the same characteristics of a wolf, like their father. He taught his sons to be warriors like him. They were ambushed at night, all four of them, but the enemy was unlike any they'd ever met.

This enemy was quick and agile, carried the copper scent of blood with claws, knifepoint fangs, and black blood. Their strength was matched with this new enemy and they fought valiantly, lopping off the heads and yanking out their hearts. The father bit into the neck and ripped out the throat of one. Its body was devoured in blackness, smoke pouring from the hole in its neck until it burst into flames.

A few days later, the father died. His sons used his bones to shape swords and knives. Their bones killed the creatures, but also cost their father's death.. Fashioning his bones into weapons they could destroy the beasts without sacrificing themselves. They went in search of their new enemy, vowing to kill each one. They named themselves Lobos de Fuego — *Wolves of fire.*

These sons also had children. The oldest had a daughter then a son with the same woman. After birthing the son, the mother died. The middle son had four boys, each of a different mother, as the women never survived birth. The youngest son had no children. He was not the fierce warrior his father and brothers were.

He and the oldest son's daughter stole to the new world. Shortly after, she met a man and married. They had a son and she died a week after his birth. The boy grew up at the monastery into a fine young man who left the monastery and married. He lost his wife when their child, a son, was born.

Distraught, his body took on a form that frightened him. His nose and face distorted into a snout, his feet and hands bore the claws of a wolf, and fur emerged all over his body, mixed with human hair. When the episode ended, he went to the monastery for help and learned the history of his family.

He raised his son hoping he would never become what he was.

Father Bornecke's face solemn, he said, "I'm the youngest son and the daughter is your grandmother." Concern and truth wrinkling on his face.

One part didn't make sense. "But I bit a Bloodseeker many years ago. I haven't died. How is this possible if I'm one of them?"

The Father's eyebrows lifted in surprise and his lips pursed in confusion. "I do not know."

That's when I decided it was time to ask. The Father seemed genuine. "I was sent here by a man." I considered my words carefully. Lars said one of *us*. "His name is Lars. He isn't a wolf. Is he a Bloodseeker?"

I knew the answer to the question by the expression on the Father's face before the words left his mouth. "Yes, but he is not like the others. He can't betray his queen openly but has a way to deceive her. He uses this to help humans. He's saved many."

There was always corruption in the highest leagues of any government or power. Someone the *queen* or *sorceress* trusted betrayed her at every turn.

A sense of knowledge embraced me. I was different to the Lobos de Fuego, as a full wolf in my change with the unique ability to bite a Bloodseeker and live. The slayer's words that I would build my army. An army of wolves. The Orators were sent to me. Together we'd build that army. That was my purpose. I saw it clearly in that moment.

chapter 14

I decided to leave in the morning since it was late when Father Bornecke and I finished our discussion. Graciously, I accepted his offer to stay the night at the monastery.

"Owyn," a voice called, waking me. Dismissing it without opening my eyes, I rolled onto my side and fell back into sleep. "Owyn," it called again. This time I didn't dismiss it as nothing more than being half awake. My eyes popped wide open and I turned towards the window.

A sliver of moon shed little light outside the window. When the voice came again, I slipped my pants on and crept through the halls quietly as if hunting and needing the element of surprise on my prey. The voice was certainly real and not a monk. It was a familiar voice.

Pushing the door open slowly to avoid it creaking, I stole into the darkness.

"Owyn." Breathy, as if carried on the wind. It was my Portencia.

I knew it couldn't be. She was dead. But the ring in the words sounded so much like her it brought feelings spilling over the surface of my heart. Was it possible she survived? I couldn't imagine how, since she barely had a heartbeat. "Portencia?"

"Over here," she called, leaves barely rustled under light feet.

I stopped at the edge of the woods. My rational side overriding my emotions. It couldn't be here, couldn't. I told myself that. A trick maybe. The Bloodseekers had attacked me once in St. Augustine, they could be planning to do it again. To be rid of the one who could kill them with one bite, yet not die in response.

I'd survived on my own too long, thought too many hours about everything. Pondered my existence to the point it was unbearable, then Sky walked into my life. She and the Orators were my life now. Standing at the tree line my wolf eyes scoured the trees and my wolf ears listened for miles. The faint thump of a heart and twist of a twig underfoot led me directly to a shadow hiding behind a tree.

This was a trick. The Bloodseekers had controlled Horacio's mind in his last moments. If they had powers to do that kind of trickery, surely they could play a simple trick with a voice. I lowered my head and stared straight at whatever it was.

"I miss you, Owyn." My Portencia wouldn't hide behind a tree. She would wrap her arms around me lovingly, waiting for me to scoop her in my arms.

"I'm here, Portencia. Where are you?" I called. Better to play the game. It would be one less Bloodseeker on the planet.

Leaves crunched underfoot like tiny snaps. It was a small foot, a woman or child. The form moved into the open between the trees and my mouth nearly dropped off my face. Her blonde hair rolling over her chest, her dainty frame, but something wasn't quite right. The clouds shifted and what little light the moon held shined on her.

It was Portencia, but not the one I'd fallen in love with. This one had sickly flesh and claws extended from her fingers. Those weren't the only tell-tale signs she was a Bloodseeker. Copper and iron eddied in the air — blood and death accompanied her.

I choked down the ball forming in my throat. My father urged me to kill Horacio to keep him from turning into one of them and so I did. I let Portencia die, thinking there was nothing I could do to save her. She was too close to death. All I had to do was sink my teeth into her flesh, instead my bride wandered the earth as a wretched Bloodseeker. Remorse and shame teemed in my heart. It was my fault. "I'm so sorry."

"We can still be together. You and I forever," she implored.

As unbearable as it was, I knew I had to do what I couldn't do all those years ago. Aware luring me into the woods was the trap, I stayed in the open. "Yes, everything will be OK now. I promise." Tears streamed my cheeks for what had to be done.

In a moment she was in front of me. Her sapphire eyes now black as her blood. I whipped my hand past my sheathed bone knife, pulling it out as I wrapped my arms around her and plunged the knife into her back.

She pushed her clawed hands against my chest, stumbling backwards, her mouth agape as smoke and flames rose from behind her. Her screams pierced the night.

chapter 15

The next morning, Amit and I started our journey home, bringing with us my father's items. It was a long journey and my own culpability and sorrow ate at me most of the trip. I would never forget that moment as flames devoured Portencia and her cries resonated in the night. But it had to be done. She was already dead and no remedy would save her from that.

I arrived at the outskirts of Wolf Manor in the afternoon, four and a half days later. As Amit and I neared the house, the front door opened wide and Sky ran down the steps and over the grass barefoot to meet us. I dismounted Amit, wrapped my arms around her and twirled her in a circle, our lips meeting in a long kiss. Her body pressed to mine, I felt the swell in her belly.

"I'm going to be a father!"

Her lips smiled, her eyes smiled as she nodded. Portencia was my first love, but Sky was my true love.

That night I tossed and turned, unsettled, the Father's words ringing in my head. My mother died in childbirth, her mother died in childbirth. They always did. What if… Sky didn't make it? I forced myself not to think that way. I was different to the Lobos de Fuego. They didn't shift into full wolves. They couldn't bite a Bloodseeker and live. I was different and Sky would live. But, if it was her time, I would raise our child as my father had, only I wasn't alone. I had the Orators.

More of them had showed in my absence. So many they'd started finishing the rooms on the third floor and the gardens were sown. Wolf Manor beamed in delight, or maybe that was me.

Sky and I married in the tradition of the Orators. She wore a tiara made of peonies, carnations, and hydrangea. She was a vision; her long, dark hair pulled up and twisted with the flowers. It was explained the flowers represented love and unity. The ceremony was simple, held on a bright spring day.

We folded our hands together and they wrapped a vine of jasmine around our hands and wrists as it signifies love, passion, and loyalty in their culture. I added a bit of my own culture and slipped a wedding band around her finger that I'd carved from the finest wood in the forest.

I refused to let my anxieties and concerns over the birth of our child destroy my time with her. I also believed in my heart the baby would be born in good health and Sky would survive, healthy and strong.

When the time came, I stayed by her side, held her hand as our son was born. His cries filling the room and my heart. They immediately laid him on her chest, flesh to flesh, and he quieted. His head covered in curly dark hair and his body so tiny I was sure it would fit in one of my hands.

Sky reached a hand over him, her eyes shifted from him to me as her hand in mine squeezed then the color drained from her face and her eyes closed. "No, Sky!" My heart dropped like lead and shattered like glass as my breath caught and my nose burned.

"Owyn, she is sleeping. She needs her rest." The midwife's words comforting. "Here." She took my hand and placed it on her chest. "You see?"

The slow but steady beat of her heart thumped against the palm of my hand. My immediate fears alleviated until the midwife spoke again.

"Birthing is hard work for one baby. Sky is having two. The other will be here soon. She needs all the rest she can get." Her words sent a second wave of horror shooting through me.

Would she survive the second child? I had to stay positive even when every part of me was filled with overwhelming dread.

The midwife's helper took our son, washed him off, and wrapped him in a cloth blanket. "Your son," she said with smiling eyes. It was as if these women had no fear.

Bringing my hands upwards she laid him in them. My eyes glued to him, I was perplexed at the little noises he made and the way he wrinkled his nose. He looked like his mother; beautiful and perfect.

"It is time, Owyn. Sky needs you again," the midwife said, breaking the trance my son put me under.

I glanced away from my son, upwards into the eyes of the midwife's helper, who held out her hands for him. I stood and carefully placed him in her arms. I felt Sky's hand on my leg and glanced down at her. She was awake.

As the second child came, I took deep breaths and repeated, *Stay calm. You are different,* in my thoughts. Another son was born as perfect as his older brother. I barely let Sky and the boys out of my sight for weeks, but eventually I understood that all were healthy, and it wasn't Sky's time.

Our boys — Ewan, the oldest, named after my father, and Shadow, as he was born second. It was fitting, as later in life he became a skillful hunter who stalked prey without a noise. Eventually, when my heart recovered from our sons' births, we tried again and again, having two daughters, Rane and Eres.

All of our children were born with the ability to shift into a wolf. They also had more control in wolf form and the ability of the Orators to speak through their minds. Over the generations, our children married and had children with the Orators and soon there were no Orators or wolves but something new — werewolves.

People continued to come, old and young, with child and with children. We built a great, thriving community. We honored their ceremonies and rituals. Our children weren't demon hunters, wolves of fire, but werewolves and, one day, we'd be large enough to destroy those I thought of as demons — the Bloodseekers.

THE VAMPIRES NEXT DOOR

The Bloodseekers Book 1
St. Augustine Novellas

Prologue

St. Augustine, 1823

Cara shivered, the stone cold floor beneath her. Shrieks sliced through the air above her, echoing through the stone walls. A moldy stench, thick in the surrounding air, drifted up her nostrils. The temperature dropped several degrees as a breeze touched her head. She dared to open her eyes and stare into the darkness surrounding her, peeling one eye open and then the next.

"Cara," sounded a soft voice, almost a whisper. A warm touch caressed her hand, a shadowy figure flashed before her eyes. "You need to leave." The soothing voice didn't elicit fear but warmth and love. Her eyes searched for whom it belonged to. A breeze brushed against her and the voice whispered in her ear. "You need to go. I can lead you."

She tilted her head and gazed upon a transparent woman, no more than twenty. Her flaxen hair fell across her shoulders, circling her heart-shaped face. "Who are you?" Cara stammered.

"I'm Alda, once like you. They've been here for centuries, before the pirates, before the first settlement. The true first inhabitants of this continent."

"Who are they?"

"They are Bloodseekers. Come now!" The urgency in her voice resounded inside Cara. She jumped to her feet and followed the apparition. Alda's white bodice hugged her torso, the black hem grazing the stone floor.

Light from candles illuminated the darkness as they wound through a narrow passageway, as one candle lit ahead of them, the one behind went dark. The brightness of each light cast a glow on the shadow beside it, lighting the faces of each ghost. One apparition after another, men and women, blood drenching their shirts and bodices from the fang marks in their necks. The chilly air sent waves of shivers spiraling through Cara's body. She lifted her arm to touch a girl, no more than twelve, but her hand went through the child's face.

They came upon a fork in the passage, Alda motioned for her to stop. Quickening footsteps sounded from the right. "Plaster yourself against the wall, into the shadows. They see heat, our lack of it will protect you."

Cara did as asked. Not questioning Alda. She knew the footsteps belonged to a Bloodseeker. One had come into her home and killed her family, draining them of every drop of blood. She tried to escape, to run,

but he was too quick. His dark eyes
bored into hers. And a voice inside
her head commanded her to stop.
Her body froze in place. She tried
to move but his mind controlled
the core of her brain and she
collapsed, waking up on the stone
floor.

Her mind swarming back to the
present, she pressed herself against
the wall, the shadowy apparitions
swarmed around her, blanketing
her in darkness, shielding her from
the Bloodseeker. His footsteps
halted at the fork, as if deliberating
which direction to go. He turned
and followed the corridor leading
to the room she'd left, he halted.
His black eyes glowed through the
shadows surrounding her. She
closed her eyes tight, to avoid his
mind commands and held her

breath. Cara stayed as motionless as possible, controlling the tremors threatening to shake her body.

Her sense of hearing heightened with her eyes squeezed shut, she heard his footsteps walk away from her and continue through the corridor. She popped her eyes open and watched his form through the corner of her eye. When he disappeared around the corner, Alda motioned for her to follow. *He'd know she wasn't there. He'd look for her.* The apparitions parted as Cara moved away from the wall.

Alda floated up the stairwell as Cara followed with gentle footsteps, careful not to draw his attention. A wooden door appeared before Cara as she reached the top of the stairs. Alda motioned for her to open it, the hinges creaking as she pushed it.

Moonlight from the crescent moon streamed through the parted heavy curtains, bathing the room in enough light that Cara could see. Dozens of ghosts swarmed the room. Now, able to see them clearly, she gasped. Their skin tones and origins varied - black, white, and varying shades of brown. None older than her. Their styles of dress told her many lived centuries before her. A young black ghost hovered in front of her, clothed in a thick graying dress. Her gentle brown eyes sent a burst of warmth through Cara's quaking, goose-pimpled body.

Alda soared towards a bookshelf and pointed to a

nondescript brown leather book. "Pull it."

Cara hurried towards the shelf and lifted the book, the shelf easing back to reveal another room.

"Take the book inside the room. The door will close behind you."

Cara didn't argue. Thundering sets of footsteps pounded the floor behind her, only moments from catching her she dived into the room. The book case closed, leaving behind all the ghosts except Alda. A Bloodseeker rushed towards it, catching it with his hand. He forced the heavy door open. Cara scooted away from his grasp.

A bright red light flickered from the corner of the dark room. "Grab the light!" Alda yelled. Cara scurried towards it, dropping the book as she reached for it. She held it firmly in her hand and tugged, but the object was caught on something she couldn't see in the dark.

The Bloodseeker dived for her, catching her other arm in his firm grasp. A blast of white light diffused through the room from the object Cara clutched in her hand. He pulled her towards him. She tightened her grasp as the object and the nail it was stuck on slackened from the wall. The Bloodseeker, too late to stop her, screamed in agony as the light blasted him against the door, his body engulfed in flames.

The light enveloped Cara, pushing its way through her body. She burst into fire, the flames licking the walls, then eddying into nothingness. Her ginger hair now crimson red, her amber eyes shining as garnets in the darkness. Beneath her skin, muscles exploded to the surface.

"What's happening?"

A smile widened on Alda's face. "You're the one. We've waited for you."

"What do you mean and how come I can see you and they can't?"

"You are a Slayer, that's why you see us. As long as you wear the amulet you will be indestructible and invisible to the Bloodseekers. They won't be able to harm you. Your job is to find others like yourself and slay every last Bloodseeker. Don't ever take it off and keep it protected beneath your clothes. Should it fall into their hands they will use it against you. You see us because you are special. All the answers are in the book. Take it, place the amulet around your neck and leave now!"

Cara leaned over and grabbed the book. She then pulled the glowing amulet over her head. "What about you and the others?"

"You have freed us. We are forever grateful but you must leave."

Cara hurried towards the door, stepping on the Bloodseeker's ashes. The door opened for her and she ran through the house, ghosts guiding her way. She dodged the Bloodseekers, their dark glowing eyes searching, fangs sharp as daggers protruding from their upper gums. Their blood covered mouths saturated the air with the scent of iron. Claw-like fingers sliced through the air, scratching her clothes as she sprinted past them, hurdling tables and furniture with skill and agility unknown to her.

Finally, reaching the front entrance, she twisted the golden knob on the large, chunky door and ran into the morning's first light. Dawn. The sun rising just above the horizon. She stepped onto the porch, Bloodseekers on her trail. Stumbling down the steps, she landed face first in the dirt. Scrambling she lifted herself upright and quickly turned towards the house.

A tall, thin Bloodseeker hissed, shielding his face as he sank into the house, flames licking his hands. The sun's light rose bigger and brighter in the sky, immersing the house in radiance. The ground shook. She sprinted.

Reaching the relative safety of the tree line, she turned in time to watch the ground part around the house, swallowing it. Thousands of lights glowed as the ghosts swirled into the atmosphere, rising high into the sky as they disappeared. Screams reverberated in the air surrounding her as the Bloodseekers were burned and buried.

She cupped her ears and knelt, curling her head towards her knees to muffle their death screeches. Unable to stifle the noise, tears rose to her eyes from the pain in her throbbing ears. As soon as the screeching began, it stopped, and the earth filled in above the house.

The ground appeared undisturbed. The sun shone high in the sky, erasing the dreadful night.

Cara lifted the amulet hanging against her chest, a large red stone set in the center surrounded by, and hanging on, a silver chain. She clutched it, the book tucked beneath her arm, and marched down the road. Not a soul peered outside their windows or took notice of the event.

The house was wiped from existence and erased from St. Augustine's inhabitants' minds. Cara's secret.

Chapter 1

Alison

Music surging from the apartment next door startled Alison awake. Her body rolled off the couch with a soft thump, landing on an assortment of throw pillows she'd kicked off during her nap. She pulled herself off the floor and rubbed the sleep from her eyes. Mouth dry as the Sahara, she headed towards the kitchen for water. A shrill female scream vibrated against her eardrums, causing her to jump and drop her empty tumbler. It crashed to the floor with a loud thunk, mimicked by the shattering glass outside her front door.

The apartment complex was always quiet, especially after dark. It had to be the new neighbors. After sunset, they'd moved into the adjoining apartment. As a lonely girl in a new city, she'd watched them with admiration. Two women, neither over the age of twenty-five, single women living on their own. One with long, brown wavy hair and eyes bluer than any she'd seen before. A surreal blue. The other girl had blonde highlights throughout the light brown hair, framing her flawless face and intense green eyes. Both had curves in the right places.

Self-conscious, she had compared her still developing body to their mature ones. Her gut swelled over her sweatpants and her chest had barely sprouted. She wore an A-cup to make herself feel better, but really she didn't think anyone noticed when she went braless. At the moment her admiration for them plummeted; beautiful or not, they were an annoyance!

Two voices, one female the other male, argued in the breezeway, the open air hallway between the apartments, upsetting her, but also piquing her natural teenage curiosity. She peered through the peephole hoping to catch sight of someone in the breezeway between the apartments but all she saw was the apartment across the hall. Her own front door blocking the view of the adjoining apartment.

"I hate you!" Then the door slammed so hard it made the walls tremble and the door shake. Alison's face pressed against the door, she yelped from the jolt against her nose. Rubbing it, she moved away and strolled back to the kitchen, picked up her tumbler and poured filtered water into it, drinking it all in several successive gulps. Catching her breath she considered her options. She could knock on their door and ask them nicely to lower their music or she could wait it out.

Home alone, as her mother worked as a nurse at Flagler hospital, and hundreds of miles from her father and best friend, she was unsure what to do, but didn't feel knocking on the door was the best choice. Actually, the idea freaked her out. Instead, she padded to the coffee table, picked up her tablet and checked the time. She was overly dismayed when her tablet screen displayed eleven p.m.

A tad scared but nosy and irritated, she slid the patio door open and listened, maybe they were wrapping up the party. All she heard was murmuring half-drowned by the music. Upset, lonely and slightly frightened she sent her BFF in Virginia a message: *I hate my life. New neighbors are crazy. I miss you.* She knew Vicky was asleep like normal people and wouldn't see her message for several more hours.

Alison laid her phone on the table and gazed towards the heavens. A chunk of moon peeked out from the surrounding clouds.

Always interested in lunar phases as most paranormal books she read featured the moon was an important piece of the story, and each phase having a specific meaning. The most well-known were the werewolves who morphed during a full moon, but red moons and blue moons had meanings too. Her body shuddered as the party next door continued, but the steady purr of a familiar vehicle kept her plastered to the chair.

Within seconds an emerald green Charger hugged the road as it passed her screened patio. Her eyes moved with it as the driver swung around the curve. She jumped from the plastic patio chair, grabbed her phone, her heart beating fast within her chest, and with a sigh, stepped inside. Almost forgetting her troublesome new neighbors. She slid the heavy glass door closed, bolting all the locks and tugging to be sure.

She raced toward the dining room window and parted the blinds, a large breezeway with philodendrons planted in the middle separated the apartments. She recognized the emerald green Dodge Charger and its driver, Rodham. To her, his chiseled body screamed for every teenage girl in a fifty mile radius to pay attention. He lived kitty corner to her apartment and directly across the hall from the new, loud neighbors.

He rounded the corner of the building, keys jingling in his hands, eyes shooting a glance across the hall towards the partying neighbors' apartment. Well defined muscles on his forearm bulged as he twisted the key in the lock. She imagined herself wrapped in those arms, his full lips kissing her neck and drifting behind her ears. Still a virgin with no prospects or past boyfriends, thoughts of Rodham filled her waking and sleeping mind. Under no circumstances did she think a hot, dreamy creature like Rodham would date an ordinary, overweight, ginger like her because she lacked the talent and looks to suck men into her web. Rodham closed the door and her moment of teenage lust ended.

Dropping the blinds, she sauntered to the fridge and lifted the papers hung on the fridge with magnets, searching for an emergency number for the apartment complex. Her mother was organized, down to every detail. As the thought brushed through her mind, she glanced at the pillows still lying on the floor and made a mental note to pick them up before bed.

With a triumphant grin, she found the number and lifted it off the fridge. Loud neighbors at eleven p.m. was an emergency in her book. She dialed the number and it directed her to leave a message. *What if I was dying? What if someone broke in and I was shivering in terror in my closet? Whatever*, she shrugged and left a message, tossed the pillows onto the couch and crawled into bed, drawing the comforter over her head, and sticking in her earbuds. She turned up the volume, attempting to drown the commotion next door and opened her tablet to her current book, *City by the Bay.*

Thirty minutes later a pounding on the front door interrupted her reading, and a shudder ran down her spine. She curled further under her covers like a frightened turtle inside its shell.

Rodham

A bottle cap skittered across the cement breezeway as Rodham rounded the corner. It landed in the dirt next to a philodendron leaf. A shattered glass bottle twinkled in the lights, its contents sprayed across the cement wall, puddling on the concrete beneath. The heavy beat from the music across the hall thumped against his eardrums.

When he drove past the apartment, he captured a glimpse of the new neighbors. Several people stood on the patio, each holding drinks in their hands. The sliding glass door open, he saw into their apartment, where a woman with blondish hair danced against a dark haired man. Her back rubbing his chest, she slid down him, her flowing hair trailing across his torso. Her partner leaned his face towards hers as she grabbed a handful of his dark hair.

Rodham fumbled with the lock, aware the apartment across the hall was empty when he'd left with his friend, Adrian, for Daytona to surf. Now, new, annoying neighbors partied and littered the breezeway.

He wondered how the quiet ginger next door was faring against the noise. Always aloof with her tablet in front of her face - at the beach, the pool, slung in a hammock on the shore of the manmade lake at the apartment complex.

Her amber eyes mysterious and deep, ginger hair trailing her back with gentle waves falling across her shoulders, freckles kissed her porcelain cheeks. Intent on her tablet, she always twisted stray strands between her fingers. From the corner of his eye he caught her amber eyes peering from her parted blinds, biting her natural cherry colored bottom lip, watching as he hurried and closed the door, locking out the new, annoying neighbors.

One finger pushed against his ear, his cell phone meshed against his other, Rodham's father acknowledged he was home with a quick flash of his eyes, then he squinted and bent over talking to the person on the other end of the line.

His mom sat, feet propped on the coffee table and plugs in her ears. Her back against the soft cushion of the sectional. Closed captioning jogged across the TV screen. She waved at him as he disappeared into his room. Beach sand stuck to every part of his body, he gathered clean clothes and rushed into the shower.

He allowed the warm water to wash the sand down the drain, the cute ginger filling his thoughts. Fully focused on her, a set of dagger-tipped fangs interrupted his thoughts. A single drop of blood hung in the air as it fell from the point of a fang. A thunderous knock blasted him out of the vision. Catching the shower's side handle to keep from slipping, he knocked the back of his head against the tile wall, hard enough to give him a temporary headache. He scurried out of the shower, both his parents' were watching something through the parted blinds.

Chapter 2

Alison

Alison yanked the earbuds out of her ears and listened. The knocking stopped, the music stopped, and muffled voices drifted through the wall. Throwing off her covers, she hurried towards the dining room window, attempting to catch a glimpse. All she saw was the black-clothed, burly back of a police officer scolding her neighbors.

"We've had complaints. This is a residential area and we're going to have to ask you to keep your music down," the officer said in a deep voice.

Across the hall, Rodham's ebony face appeared through parted blinds. His sable eyes met her amber orbs locking them in a gaze. *He noticed me!* Thought Alison, the ambiguous girl whom he hadn't paid one ounce of attention to all summer. Warmth tingled through her body and she all but forgot about her matted bed-head, and Tinker Bell pajamas. The expanded-second locked gaze ended, and he dropped his blinds back in place.

She twirled her body away from the window and, in a dreamy state, leaned against the wall, thoughts of the day she followed him to the beach, flitted through her head. She'd poised her chair under an umbrella, sprayed SPF 130 over her entire pale body, placed a floppy hat on her head and watched him with stars in her eyes from behind the pages of her book while pretty girls with dream bodies in their bikinis flocked towards him like bees to honey. His brown skin velvet beneath the sun. She pushed her book, *Beyond the Hidden Sky*, over her face and read, catching glimpses of Rodham. In her one-piece with a baggy T-shirt to cover her jelly stomach she didn't think she compared to the other teens.

She peeled herself off the wall and strolled to her bedroom. *He noticed me!* Sinking into her bed she savored our moment in her mind, silence next door - she fell asleep.

Sun filtering through her window awoke her the following morning. She crept towards her mother's room, peeking around the corner of her opened door. She lay on her bed, burrito-wrapped inside the covers, feet poking out the end. Alison sighed relief that her mother was home. She'd grown used to her absence at night and had felt safe enough until last night.

Her stomach grumbling for food, she strolled into the kitchen, poured a bowl of cereal and ate while she turned on her tablet and continued reading her current book.

Hours later, her mother stretched her arms as she exited her bedroom and ambled into the kitchen. With a yawn she said, "Good afternoon, sweetie."

Peeling her eyes from her tablet and current fictional world, Alison acknowledged her mother from her prone position on the couch and lifted her eyes responding, "Hi, Mom. I fixed lunch, frozen lasagna and garlic bread."

"What did I ever do to get such a wonderful daughter?" She spied Alison's tablet. "I love all the reading you do. It helps the mind grow, but I hate seeing you inside all day, every day. That's why we bought you the car so you could get out, explore your new surroundings, meet new people. This is St. Augustine, the oldest city in the U.S., there's more than enough to keep you busy and entertained." She gently pushed Alison's legs towards the back cushion of the couch and sat, pecking her on the cheek.

Alison's parents had bought her a 2000 Corolla, not a bad first car. In fact, she thought it was an excellent first car - everything worked. The problem was they lived in Florida and she detested starting the car and setting the air conditioning to full blast for ten minutes before she could sit in it without melting or touch the steering wheel without second degree burns.

Her next problem was the friend issue. As an introverted book nerd, it took her years to build the relationships she had - Vicky, she was it. Her only friend. She anticipated she'd be spending the two years left of high school alone.

Alison's phone vibrated and she glanced at the message, Vicky responding to her late night text. *Miss you! Talk later, school shopping.* She wished she was in Virginia shopping with her, the way they'd done the past few years, since their parents deemed them old enough to wander the mall without 24/7 parental supervision.

"I miss Vicky, my high school, the mountains, the cooler night air."

Her mother sighed and brushed her hand through Alison's hair. "Honey, I know this is difficult for you. But your dad travels a lot. I was offered a job here. This is our home now. School starts next week, try and make friends."

"I know. I'll try." She bit her lower lip. "And when the weather gets cooler I'll explore the city." After her parents' divorce, her mother, who'd spent sixteen years as a stay at home mom, dusted off her nursing degree and sent her resume all over the U.S., hoping to land a job. She did, in St. Augustine, to Alison's bad fortune.

Her mother stood and wandered towards the kitchen, cutting a slice of lasagna and placing it on a plate, then sighed as she popped it in the microwave. "I've been working a lot, paying moving expenses. Once they're paid up we'll do more exploring together."

Facing away from her mother, Alison rolled her eyes and shrugged, the only exploring they'd done together was watching an IMAX movie at World Golf Village. And it was an excellent outing but, other than that, her mother constantly worked. Alison was old enough to understand child support didn't pay everything. She also understood her parents continued an amiable relationship if nothing else than for her, and her father would do more to help them out. Her mother, proud and stubborn, refused any money other than the court dictated amount.

She contemplated telling her mother about the neighbors but chose against it, assuming it was a one-night thing.

As soon as the sun went down, the neighbors' thumping music and partying began, growing louder as the night progressed. She built up the nerve to walk to her front door, replaying what she would say in her mind. As she turned the knob she chickened out, her anger inside recoiled and she stuck her earbuds in and read instead.

After midnight a thump hit her bedroom wall, she leaped off the couch in response. The decorative Asian fan above the couch shifted. Several more thumps followed, sounding like a body thrown against the wall. She stood in the doorway, expecting someone to burst through the wall any second. A shrill banshee scream shuddered through the air, piercing her eardrums, and vibrating through her head. In pain, Alison crumpled to the ground, holding her head between her hands.

Frozen in pain, she gripped the floor and dragged her body along it to the couch, reached her hand onto the cushion and fumbled for her phone. Then the noise stopped. Her fingers brushed against her phone and she snatched it up.

Poised on the floor, she scrolled through her short phone log and redialed the emergency number then buried herself into the couch, encasing her fear-shivering body in a throw blanket.

Rodham

At the same moment, in his room playing Wii, a primitive wail sliced through the music, ringing in Rodham's ears. He doubled in pain, and curled into a ball, dropping the video game controller from his hand.

When the noise subsided, Rodham collected himself. Unable to shrug it off, he contemplated where the noise originated.

Thoughts of his strange neighbors and the odd events, including his strange visions, circulated in his head.

In the living room, he joined his parents. Their eyes fixed on the TV as they watched a movie, closed captioning scrolling across the screen. Noticing her son's befuzzled look, his mother asked, "Everything OK?"

He shifted his eyes to hers. "Did you hear that?"

His father chuckled. "Two nights in a row. I've already called the sheriff and will make a complaint at the office in the morning."

Rodham shrugged and leaned back into the recliner, convinced his parents didn't hear the shrill scream or couldn't hear it over the pulsating music. In science class he learned that young adults were capable of hearing frequencies adults ears couldn't.

Within a half hour a police officer knocked on their neighbor's door, read them the "be quiet" act and the noise stopped.

The following two nights, the neighbors' partying after sunset continued. Determined to understand the strange sequence of events, Rodham slipped upstairs to the second floor balcony, found a dark corner and waited. He wanted to know, see everything. His visions and the noise told him something was very wrong. No matter how absurd it sounded, even inside his own head, his curiosity drove him forward.

The crackle of the police radio hummed before he saw the two officers. Within moments a female officer with a blonde bob cut and wide hips, along with a male, his paunchy gut swelling over his pants, rounded the corner. The man slipped a piece of chewing gum into his mouth, stuffing the wrapper into his pants and chomped, his high and tight hair style moved up and down with the motion.

They knocked on the door and a woman with blonde highlights contrasting against her brown hair opened it. She leaned against the door frame, her long legs flowing like silk from her short denim skirt. "Hello officers."

"Ma'am, four nights in a row we've been called to this location for the same reason. I think we need to have a discussion with you and your roommate." His head bobbed as he glanced around her at the inside of the apartment. From Rodham's position he couldn't see inside but not willing to give away his position, he stayed put.

A crooked, sinister smile crossed her oval face, and she waved the officers inside. Her eyes darted right then left, scoping the breezeway before she closed the door.

In the dark corner, Rodham waited. The music stopped, but he never saw the police leave. Fear rushed against his spine, and he leaped down the stairs, taking two at a time, and thrust his front door open. His parents looked at him wearing identical expressions of puzzlement. He ignored them, locked the door, and parted the blinds enough to peek out with one eye.

"What's going on?" questioned his father, as he walked towards him.

"Police are here again, two of them tonight. They went inside the apartment."

"Young, irresponsible, spoiled girls is all. Their parents probably pay for the apartment to get them out of their own home." He harrumphed. "Now that the noise has stopped we're heading to bed."

"Goodnight, don't stay up too late," called his mother as she trailed to bed.

"Goodnight," answered Rodham, his eye still fixated on the apartment across the hall.

He knew from the tone in his father's voice he questioned his actions, but not enough to figure them out after four near-sleepless nights.

Their neighbor's blinds were parted slightly, allowing him to see the woman with highlighted hair, the one who opened the door, stared into the male officer's eyes and brushed her fingers against his neck. She opened her mouth, fangs erupted from her gums. Rodham's eyes widened as he watched the man's blood vessels bulge from beneath his skin and pulsate as his blood pumped through his arteries. She tilted her head and sunk her fangs into his flesh, a drop of blood trailed down his neck, and under his shirt.

Her eyes shifted towards Rodham, who stumbled backwards and blinked his eyes, the blinds falling into place. His heartbeat steady and fast inside his chest and he struggled to catch his breath.

www.ingramcontent.com/pod-product-compliance
Lightning Source LLC
Chambersburg PA
CBHW021146190726
48288CB00008B/2842